Jim Henson's THE DARK CRYSTAL AGE OF RESISTANCE

AUGHRA'S WISDOM of THRA

PENGUIN YOUNG READERS LICENSES
An Imprint of Penguin Random House LLC, New York

Published in 2019 by Penguin Young Readers Licenses, an imprint of
Penguin Random House LLC, New York. Manufactured in China.

Visit us online at www.penguinrandomhouse.com.

ISBN 9780593094327   10 9 8 7 6 5 4 3 2 1

Jim Henson's THE DARK CRYSTAL
AGE OF RESISTANCE

AUGHRA'S
WISDOM of THRA

BY J. M. LEE

ILLUSTRATED BY CORY GODBEY

THERE IS MUCH TO KNOW IN THIS WORLD,

and even more

to *not* know.

IF THE ROCK RUNS AWAY FROM YOU, CHASE IT;

but if it moves not,
leave it alone.

CLOSE YOUR MOUTH
BEFORE AND AFTER SAYING ANYTHING.

Otherwise you never know
what might come out . . .

or fly in.

IF YOU SIT
IN THE RIVER,
NO ONE
WILL NOTICE.

Especially not the river.

THE SUNS HAVE NO EARS TO HEAR YOUR PRAYERS,
THE MOONS NO EYES TO SEE YOUR TEARS,
THE STARS NO MOUTH TO TELL YOUR FORTUNE.

They do
not know
the answers.

ONCE SOMEONE'S DEAD,

they could be
anywhere.

ONCE YOU'VE EATEN HALF A SLUG,

might as well swallow the rest of it.

NEVER ASK
WHAT'S IN THE
CAULDRON.

IF IT LOOKS LIKE IT AND SMELLS LIKE IT,

maybe it is.

LIFE
IS
SHORT

and

dreadfully,

tiresomely,

exhaustingly,

unbelievably

LONG.

NO PLACE TO PUT IT?
Don't try to move it.

END.
BEGIN.

All the same.

AND IF YOU
FIND YOURSELF
LOST
OR *AT A LOSS*,
REMEMBER:

Sometimes
you don't know.

Sometimes
you *just*
don't know.

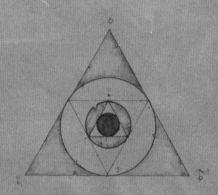